For Laura

This book belongs to:

_____

A catalogue record for this book is available from the British Library

Published by Ladybird Books Ltd Loughborough Leicestershire UK
Ladybird Books is a subsidiary of the Penguin Group of companies

Text and illustrations © Chris Demarest MCMXCV
© LADYBIRD BOOKS LTD MCMXCV
This edition MCMXCVI
LADYBIRD and the device of a Ladybird are trademarks of Ladybird Books Ltd

Benedict
goes to the beach

by Chris Demarest

Ladybird

It was hot in the city. Too hot for Benedict. "I'm going to the beach," he said.

"But it's too hot to fly!" moaned his brothers and sister. "We're not coming."

"Fine. I'll go on my own," said Benedict
huffily. And off he flew.

In no time at all he spotted some big umbrellas. "This beach is very crowded," thought Benedict.

"It's much too noisy… and there's no sand."

So off he flew.

"Ah," sighed Benedict. "A quiet spot…

...and what nice sand."

But this beach moved.

VAROOM! And Benedict tumbled off.

Then Benedict spotted some seagulls.
"They'll help me find a beach,"
he thought.

But the seagulls ignored him.

And anyway...

...their beach stank. PHEW-EE!

Poor Benedict was hotter than ever.
He was having no luck at all, until...

...he spotted a giant fish. Surely a fish
would know the way to the beach.
So off he flew.

But this fish would have nothing to do
with Benedict.

It swooped and spiralled. Then it
swatted Benedict with its tail. Down
he tumbled…

...*KERPLONK!*
Right on to his brothers' and
sister's blanket.

"You were right, Benedict," they sang.
"The beach is the place to be. We've
been waiting for you!"

Benedict beamed and wiggled his toes in the sand. He was happy and cool at last.

Then they all ate… and played…
and swam…

...until it was time to sail home.